ISBN 1 85854 469 6
© Brimax Books Ltd 1996. All rights reserved.
Published by Brimax Books Ltd, Newmarket,
CB8 7AU, England 1996.
Printed in China.

Teddy's Tail

by Lucy Kincaid
Illustrated by Peter Rutherford

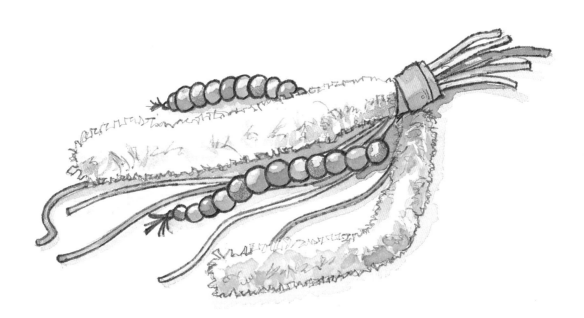

BRIMAX • NEWMARKET • ENGLAND

Lion

Lion has a swinging tail.

Monkey

Monkey has a long tail.

Dog

Dog has a wagging tail.

Horse

Horse has a swishing tail.

Raccoon

Raccoon has a bushy tail.

Kangaroo

Kangaroo has a strong tail.

Teddy is sad.

Teddy does not have a tail.

Teddy is happy.

Teddy has made his own tail.